DEDICATIO

To my family and my friends who suppor

The Case of the Disappearing Yarn

Charlotte Mae Mokry

Shannon L. Mokry

Published by: Sillygeese Publishing, LLC

Sillygeese Publishing, LLC
P. O. Box 1434
Elgin, TX 78621
info@sillygeesepublishing.com

ISBN: 9781951521882

CONTENTS

1

The Yarn Disappears

Rose was standing in the craft room in her house, trying to decide what color yarns she should use to teach Melanie how to knit. Her mom had told her to pick any color and make it into a ball of yarn for Melanie, her BFF. It sounded easy until she saw how many different colors of yarn her mother had. There were reds, blues, purples, and even some pinks!

"What color should we use, Mom?" Rose called. She was holding a pink and a purple in her hands.

"You decide…" her mom called back.

Then the doorbell rang.

"I got it!" Rose yelled. With the two colors still in her hands, she raced to let her friend in.

Tucking one color under her elbow, she swung open the door.

"Melanie!"

"Rose!"

The girls squealed each other's names, and Rose dropped both yarns as they hugged.

Jerry, Melanie's little brother, picked them up, and went to the craft room, but no one seemed to notice.

"Melanie, come and pick out the color for your scarf." Rose jumped right to the purpose of their play date. "Where did the yarn I had go?"

Just then Jerry came back without the yarn. "I put it in your craft room. Let's go outside and play." Jerry was full of energy.

"Thank you, Jerry," Melanie told her little brother.

"Are you girls going to let me in?" Melanie's mom asked.

"Sorry, Mom," Melanie said as Rose grabbed her hand and dragged her to the craft room. "I guess we are starting with knitting, Jerry, so why don't you go out and play with your ball…"

"Now, what color yarn would you like?" Rose was back on task.

"Show me the colors you had picked out," Melanie replied.

Rose quickly located the pink and purple she had been holding earlier. They were on the floor, and Rose's fluffy grey cat, Mr. Whiskers, was sniffing them.

"I'll take the purple one," Melanie decided.

"Then I'll have the pink one," Rose said. "Give me just a minute while I roll up your ball," she told her friend, then grabbed the purple yarn and quickly turned it into a ball. "Now where did I put the knitting needles?"

Melanie shrugged, and Rose spotted them in a jar on her mother's cutting table.

They sat down, and Rose started to explain how to knit. It took several tries, and Melanie started to get frustrated.

"Let's watch a video in slow motion and see if that helps," Rose suggested, "That really helped me."

Rose grabbed her tablet and pulled up a video of a person teaching knitting in slow motion. It took several more tries, but once Melanie finally got the hang of it, it was easy peasy after all.

Rose and Melanie were still knitting when Rose's mom called them for a snack. They quickly dropped their knitting and ran to the table.

Jerry came in for his snack too. He finished his apple slices before Rose and Melanie, but didn't stay long. The second he was done, he ran out of the room.

"Your brother has way to much energy!" Rose told Melanie, while shaking her head.

Melanie just smiled in agreement.

When the two girls came back to finish their knitting, it was missing.

"What happened to the yarn?" Rose asked, not executing an answer..

Melanie looked around, "And our needles?"

"Ugh, this happens all the time…"grumbled Rose.

"Do you know who's doing it?" Melanie asked.

Rose shook her head and said, "No! And it's so frustrating!"

"Then, this sounds like a job for Detectives Melanie and Rose," Melanie told her friend. They stopped looking for a moment and grinned at each other.

Just then, Rose's dog, Ruffbert, walked in, carrying his leash in his mouth. Rose ignored him and went back to looking for her yarn. Melanie got down on the floor and looked under the couch.

"Grrmph." Ruffbert tried to bark at them for attention.

"Rose have you taken Ruffbert for a walk yet?" Rose's mom asked from the other room.

"No," Rose sighed, "I suppose I should."

"What if we discuss the case while we walk," Melanie suggested.

"Yeah, that will make the walk less boring," Rose agreed, then grabbed a notebook and pencil from her detective's briefcase.

"Ooh, cool briefcase," Melanie told her friend.

"Yeah, Mom got it for me, to keep our case files in," Rose said, trying to sound serious, then ruined it by giggling.

"Grrmph," Ruffbert tried again.

"NOW, ROSE!" her mom called to her again.

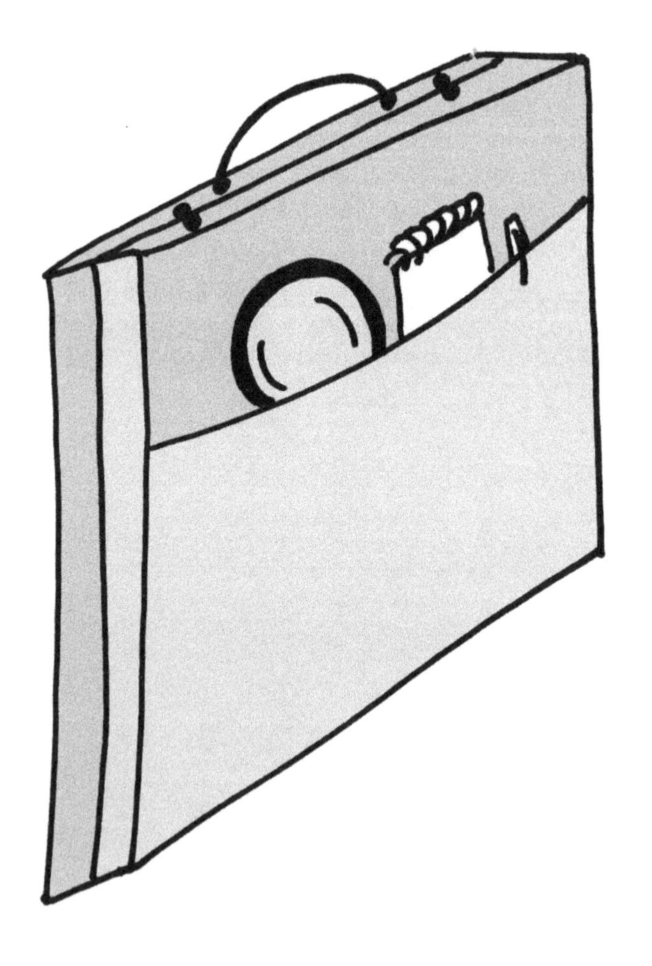

2

The File

Rose handed Melanie the notebook as she clipped Ruffbert's leash on his collar. After making it outside, Melanie flipped open the notebook.

"What should we name this case?" Melanie asked, trying to be serious again. "How about 'The Case of the Invisible Yarn'."

"No, the yarn isn't invisible, it keeps going missing," Rose said.

"Same thing, isn't it?" Melanie asked.

"No, not at all. If it was invisible, it would still be there, but its NOT there at all," Rose said.

"Well hmmm. 'The Case of the …'" Melanie trailed off thinking.

"It's 'The Case of the Disappearing Yarn'," Rose finally said.

"That's a good name!" Melanie agreed.

"Now tell me more about all the times that the yarn has disappeared, so I can make list," Melanie said.

"Great idea, because a list can help us decide who our suspects are," Rose said. "Let's see, hmm… it started when Mom decided to teach me how to knit, about a month ago. The first time it happened, Mom and I took a hot cocoa break."

Melanie wrote down everything that Rose said. "How do you spell cocoa?" Melanie tapped the pencil on her cheek.

"C-O-C-A-O?" Rose answered.

"No, that looks wrong… Oh well, we can fix it later. When was the next event?" Melanie asked.

"When you came over and I set down my knitting to play. That was a couple of weeks ago," Rose told her.

Ruffbert barked at them. He was ready to head home.

They headed back, and Melanie kept listing the times that Rose could remember the yarn coming up missing.

At home they picked out a file to hold the case notes. This time the file was purple, Melanie's favorite color. In big black letters, Rose wrote the 'THE CASE OF THE DISAPPEARING YARN.'

"What now, do we work on the case or find our yarn?" Melanie asked.

Before Rose could answer, Melanie's mom yelled, "Time to go!"

"Five more minutes, Mom? We need to find my yarn so I can practice." Melanie called back to her.

"Okay, but not a minute longer," her mom responded. "We have to get Jerry to his appointment."

"Another appointment, what's wrong with your brother?" Rose whispered.

"What isn't wrong with him?" Melanie whispered back, but giggled.

"I found a knitting needle!" Rose held it up triumphantly.

"Okay, but doesn't it take two?" Melanie laughed at her friend.

"Oh, yeah." Rose scowled and kept looking.

When the five minutes was up, they still only had one needle, but they trooped over to the front door, shoulders sagging. Melanie's mom was getting Jerry from the back yard.

"Good bye," they both said at once.

"Wow, that was creepy!" Jerry said as he ran up, waving another knitting needle.

"Hey, where did you get that?" Rose asked distrustfully.

"It was on the floor by the back door. I almost stepped on it. Mom said to bring it to you." Jerry handed it over to Rose.

"Did you see any yarn?" Melanie asked her brother.

"No, just the stick." Jerry smiled.

"Well, I guess I need to look outside the craft room," Rose said. Then the two girls hugged and said good bye again.

"C'mon, I'll get you some yarn after the appointment," Melanie's mom said as she ushered them out the door.

3

It's Always Jerry

Rose went back to the craft room to get her briefcase. She took it to the dinner table so she could snack and think. Rose was swinging her legs as she often did, when she felt her foot kick something. Looking down, under the table she saw a trail of pink yarn.

Excitedly, she pulled her magnifying glass out of her briefcase and got down on the floor. She followed the trail of pink yarn until it ended next to the purple ball of yarn and Jerry's soccer ball. He must have forgotten it.

Picking up the yarn, she inspected it. The knitting was all torn out, and the needles were missing. The purple ball of yarn was like that, too.

Rose sat back down and picked up her pencil.

"What have I learned so far?" Rose whispered to herself. "I found one needle, Jerry found the other. The pink yarn was next to the purple yarn and… Jerry's soccer ball, but it started under Jerry's chair. Hmmm."

	Suspect #1 : JERRY
	Access: Today when he kept popping in and out of rooms by himself.
1	Specifically, he left the snack table and disappeared.
2	He found a knitting needle when no one else could.
3	He . . .
	Motive: To cause mischief, that is what he DOES!
	Proof: It's always Jerry!!!

Rose's mom wondered into the room. "Oh, you found the yarn, both balls, too!" She glanced over Rose's shoulder and saw what she had written. "Rose, I really don't think it could have been Jerry. He's such a sweet boy. Also, he wasn't here last time."

"Or, that's what he wants us to think." Rose mumbled and glared at the notebook.

"What, Rose?" her mom asked.

"Nothing!" Rose continued to glare at her notebook but flipped a page to start a new list. That seemed to make her mom happy.

The next morning Rose got up and ran downstairs. Melanie was coming back over, so she wanted to review her case facts one more time. She thought, "What could be number 3?" Melanie wouldn't take Jerry as a real suspect without more evidence.

"What if I set up the dinner table for questioning Jerry?" Rose asked no one in particular. Which was good, because no one was in the room with her.

"Mom, do we have any lamps or flashlights I can borrow?!" Rose yelled to her mom.

"You know where they are, take what you need," Rose's mom responded.

Rose went and got a flashlight, a lamp, and pulled the curtains closed. She was ready for Jerry's next visit. Er, for Melanie's next visit.

"Mom, when will Melanie get here?" Rose asked impatiently.

"Before lunch, dear," Rose's mom answered.

Rose sighed and got out her a notebook again.

Interragation Questions

1. Where were you during snack time, yesterday?
2. You were in the craft room alone, right?
3. Where were you Monday, three weeks ago, at 3pm?
4. Did anyone else see you find the knitting needle?
5. Why was the yarn under your seat?

4

The Interrogation

The doorbell rang.

"Rose can you get the door?" her mom called to her.

"Already there!" Rose responded as she opened the door.

"Rose!"

"Melanie!"

The two girls yelled and hugged.

"Where is your brother?" Rose asked.

"Tell your mom thanks, I gotta run." Melanie's mom interrupted that line of questioning, and Jerry ran past and up the stairs.

"Okay, bye." Rose closed the door and dragged Melanie to the bottom of the stairs with her. "Jerry, want to play with us?" Rose called up to him.

Ruffbert ran down the stairs and out the back door.

"Hey, what was that in Ruffbert's mouth?" Melanie asked, as she stared after the dog.

Rose shrugged and called up to Jerry again.

She could here a muffled shout of"YES!" and the faint sound of something falling. An alarmed expression crossed over Melanie's face.

Rose closed her eyes and took a deep breath, then smiled and acted like this was normal.

Jerry came skidding down the hallway to the top of the stairs holding a knitting needle.

"Look what I found."

"Thanks, Jerry," Melanie said as he came down the stairs.

"Come on, lets go play in the dining room," Rose said, ushering them in that direction.

"Alright!" Jerry said, jumping around as they headed into the other room.

"Are you really Rose? Your not an alien disguised as Rose, are you?" Melanie whispered to her friend.

"If I am, I've got a really good plan, and you'll never know," Rose whispered back and winked at Melanie.

As they enter to dining room, Rose switched off the light. The room was now dark except for the one lamp shining directly onto Jerry's favorite chair.

"Take a seat, Jerry," Rose said.

Melanie's jaw dropped.

Rose grabbed her friend and quickly whispered."You're the good cop, I'm the bad cop."

"What are you doing?" Melanie whispered back, afraid she knew what was happening, but not sure what to do about it.

Jerry smiled and sat down down. Rose picked up her notebook and pencil from the table.

"We are going to play a little game called interrogation." Rose smiled. Melanie frowned.

"Question one. Where where you during snack time, yesterday?" Rose asked.

"Right here, with you," Jerry answered.

"Wrong, you left before we did. Where did you go?"

"She means, can you please tell us where you went 'after' you finished your snack?" Melanie quickly spoke up. "Be nice, or my mom will hear about it," Melanie whispered.

"I'm bad cop, your good cop," Rose whispered back.

"Out back. I was kicking my ball and chasing your chickens."

"Speaking of which," Rose said, "I found your ball. It's by the front door now. I also found some yarn next to it. Any idea why that might be?"

"Can we go play ball now? This isn't fun." Jerry jumped out of his seat.

"How about we play ball after we play interrogation?" Rose pasted a smile back on her face.

Melanie took the notebook from her friend and turned on the light. "Why don't I do the interrogating now?"

Jerry frowned and crossed his arms. "I want to be the integrator. What is an integrator?"

Rose pretended she didn't hear the last part. " You can be the interrogator next time."

Melanie frowned at the list of questions. " Just one more question, Jerry," Melanie toldhim. She put down the notebook and sat down with her brother.

"I'm hungry, are you?"

Jerry brightened back up, "YES!"

"Rose, what's for lunch today?"

Rose gave her friend a frustrated look. "Pizza. But mom hasn't cooked it yet."

"My turn first then," Jerry says.

"Ask me anything then, Jerry," his sister offered.

"Do you know what I'm allergic too?" Jerry asked very seriously.

"Umm, tomatoes," Melanie answered.

Jerry nodded.

"Can I have pizza?" he asked her.

"Ummmm. No," Melanie responded.

Jerry nodded again.

Rose's mom walked in.

"Mom, Jerry can't have pizza," Rose let her mom know.

"Don't worry, I have a special pizza for Jerry and me with no tomatoes." Rose's mom smiled at Jerry. "Why is it so dark in here?" She pulled open the curtains. Lunch won't be for a while. Why don't you kids go outside to play?"

"Yay, you promised we'd go play ball." Jerry jumped and raced to get his ball.

Rose sighed., "the things I do for the truth."

That interrogation hadn't gone as planned, but she had learned something.

5

Mr. Whiskers

Rose hung her head as they headed out to play ball with Jerry.

Melanie noticed Rose drooping.

"Cheer up, we only have to play a couple of rounds with my brother, then we can get back on the case," Melanie said, trying to comfort her friend as they walked out the door.

"I suppose…" Rose replied.

"Come on, let's play!" Jerry yelled from the backyard.

"We're coming, Jerry!" Melanie yelled back.

A few minutes later, the two girls walked out the back door, stepping around Mr. Whiskers as he headed inside. *Smart cat*, thought Rose.

"Finally!" Jerry complained and kicked the ball at them.

"Careful, you could have hit Mr. Whiskers," Rose said grumpily.

Melanie kicked the ball back, and the game began.

Rose suddenly took off running trying to intercept the ball before Jerry could get it. If Rose was going to play with Jerry, it was going to be a exciting game…

As they were kicking the ball around, it went pphhphphffft as it flattened.

The loud pphhphphffft noise was the air as it suddenly escaped the ball. Rose and Melanie looked at each other oddly, then jogged over to see what had happened to Jerry's ball.

They found it flat with a knitting needle sticking out of it.

"I guess the knitting needle punctured the ball," Melanie said.

"I think that is the last of the missing knitting needles," Rose said as she nodded.

"What's it doing out here? And why?" Melanie wondered.

"I don't know, good question, Detective Melanie," Rose replied. Then she turned to Jerry, half happy, but pretending to be sad. "I guess the game is over."

"Let's go see if lunch is ready," Melanie suggested.

Rose picked up the ball and the knitting needle. She would inspect it for clues later.

"More proof that Jerry had the opportunity for taking the yarn," Rose whispered as she pulled the needle out of the ball.

"Wasn't your cat just out here sniffing around?" Melanie whispered back.

"I suppose you're right."

"If Jerry is a suspect, so is Mr. Whiskers, and the cat has access 24/7," Melanie said.

Both girls looked at each other in frustration, then they all trooped back inside.

"Ah, perfect timing, I was just about to go and get you. Lunch is ready," Rose's mom told them.

"Good, I'm starving," Jerry said.

"Your brother is so dramatic," Rose whispered to Melanie.

"I know, right." Melanie giggled.

Rose set down the ball and knitting needle so she could get her pizza. Then she joined everyone as they sat around the table.

"My ball is flat. It went pphhphphffft," Jerry told Rose's mom as she sat next to him for lunch.

"Jerry, not at the table," Rose's mom said.

The girls giggled.

"No, Mooom, that is the noise the ball made when it went flat," Rose said.

"Still, not at the table. He was spitting everywhere," Rose's mom said.

Jerry smiled and made the pphhphphffft noise again.

"Jerry." Rose's mom looked at him severely but dropped the subject. "What caused the ball to go flat?"

"We accidentally kicked into into the last missing knitting needle," Melanie told her.

"But at least we now have two sets of knitting needles again, so we can practice some more," Rose told here.

"But what if they go missing again?" Melanie replied between mouthfuls of pizza.

"Why don't we make a list of where all the missing knitting supplies have been found?" Rose suggested.

"Great idea," Melanie agreed.

Rose shoved the rest of her pizza in her mouth, then grabbed her notebook and pencil.

Rose's mom narrowed her eyes at Rose for that move with the pizza, but she just shrugged her shoulders and started the list.

Needle 1: craft room-Rose
Needle 2: back door-Jerry
2 balls of yarn, dining room-Rose
Needle 3: ...
Needle 4:

"Hey Jerry, where did you find the needle earlier?" Melanie asked her brother.

"On the cat tree, outside Rose's bedroom." Jerry answered while chewing his pizza.

Rose glared at him, and wrote down the location.

Needle 3: Upstairs cat tree-Jerry
Needle 4: Backyard-ball

Melanie peeked over Rose's shoulder and giggled, then said, "See, it had to be Mr. Whiskers."

"We don't have any hard evidence," Rose replied.

"Same thing for Jerry," Melanie whispered.

"Well, I do think we still have some missing needles, but for now, why don't you and Melanie go practice your knitting?" Rose's mom suggested as she stood up and gathered the dirty dishes.

6

It Can't Be Ruffbert

They heard Ruffbert come in through the doggy door behind them. A moment later he was sniffing their toes.

"Ruffbert!" Rose giggled.

"Did you remember to feed, Ruffbert?" Rose's mom asked.

"Nooo…" Rose signed.

Ruffbert put his paws on the table and sniffed at the knitting needle. Then he dropped back to the floor and gave Jerry a sad look. Peeking quickly at Rose's mom, he dropped a piece of crust for the dog.

"Now, Rose." Her mom's tone got firm. "Jerry, we don't feed Ruffbert people food," she added without skipping a beat.

Jerry's face fell. "Sorry, boy," he told Ruffbert and picked up his pizza crust from the floor."

Rose got up and went over to pantry and scooped out his food. Then poured it into his food dish.

"Ruffbert, here boy." Rose called.

Rose waited for Ruffbert to start eating, then the two girls headed to the craft room

Melanie grabbed the knitting needle off the end of the table.

"We will try to patch the ball when we get home tonight, okay, Jerry?" Melanie told her brother.

"He can use Rose's ball for now," Rose's mom added.

"But…" Rose tried to object, but Melanie grabbed her arm and dragged her into the hallway.

Half way to the craft room, Ruffbert met them with his leash in his mouth.

"Grrmph," Ruffbert tried to bark.

"Rose!" her mom called from the kitchen.

"What, Mom?" Rose replied, her shoulders drooping again.

"Did you forget to walk Ruffbert this morning again?" Rose's mom responded.

"How did she know?" Melanie wondered.

"Moms are psychic." Rose answered.

"I'm taking him now, Mom." Rose called as she clicked on the leash.

On the way out the door, Melanie dropped the knitting needle into a basket.

Halfway down the block, Rose smacked herself on the forehead. "I forgot the detective notebook, and I was going to add Mr. Whiskers as a suspect."

"I have a notecard," Melanie offered, pulling a crumpled notecard from her pocket. "And a pencil." She held up her half inch long pencil.

"That is one short pencil," Rose giggled.

"I know, it's my favorite." Melanie grinned back.

Smoothing out the card, Melanie tried to write:

Suspect #2 : Mr. whiskers

Access: 24/7

1 While Rose was drinking hot chocolate with her mom

2 Cat door stuff inside back door and in backyard

3 Cat tree

Motive: To play, cause he's a CAT

Proof: ... locations of knitting needles?

"We have Jerry, and we have Mr. Whiskers. Who else could it be?" Melanie asked.

"Ruff, ruff." Ruffbert pulled at his leash.

"Is he done?" Melanie asked.

"I think so," Rose decided. "I wasn't really paying attention, but if *he* wants to go home, then home we go."

"Seriously now, any other suspects?" Melanie asked.

"I mean, who else could it be?" Rose answered.

"Ruff, ruff." Ruffbert answered.

"I wish I could understand the dog. Maybe he has a suspect for us," Rose complained as she opened the house door. After they all made into the entryway, Rose unclipped his leash.

"Wouldn't that be great! But then we wouldn't have all fun figuring it out," Melanie said.

Just then, Ruffbert grabbed the knitting needle from the basket and raced to the back door.

"Ruffbert, drop it!" Rose yelled as she ran after him. Melanie stood stunned by the door.

Rose picked up the knitting needle and headed back to Melanie.

"I know, maybe your dog did it," Melanie said, thoughtfully.

"No way, he's too sweet," Rose disagreed.

"Let's make him a suspect anyway. Then our moms might let me spend the night to prove it," Melanie suggested.

Melanie smoothed out the notecard again on the table next to the door and quickly wrote:

Suspect #3 : Ruffbert

Access: 24/7

1 Same as Mr. Whiskers

2 ???....

3

Motive: frame Mr. Whiskers (dun dun duuuun)

Proof: ... none, he's an awesome dog.

"Fine, now let's get some knitting done," Melanie said. "Mom will be back soon, and I want them to see we are doing other stuff. My mom likes to see me make progress on my projects."

"Yours and mine too," Rose replied, rolling her eyes.

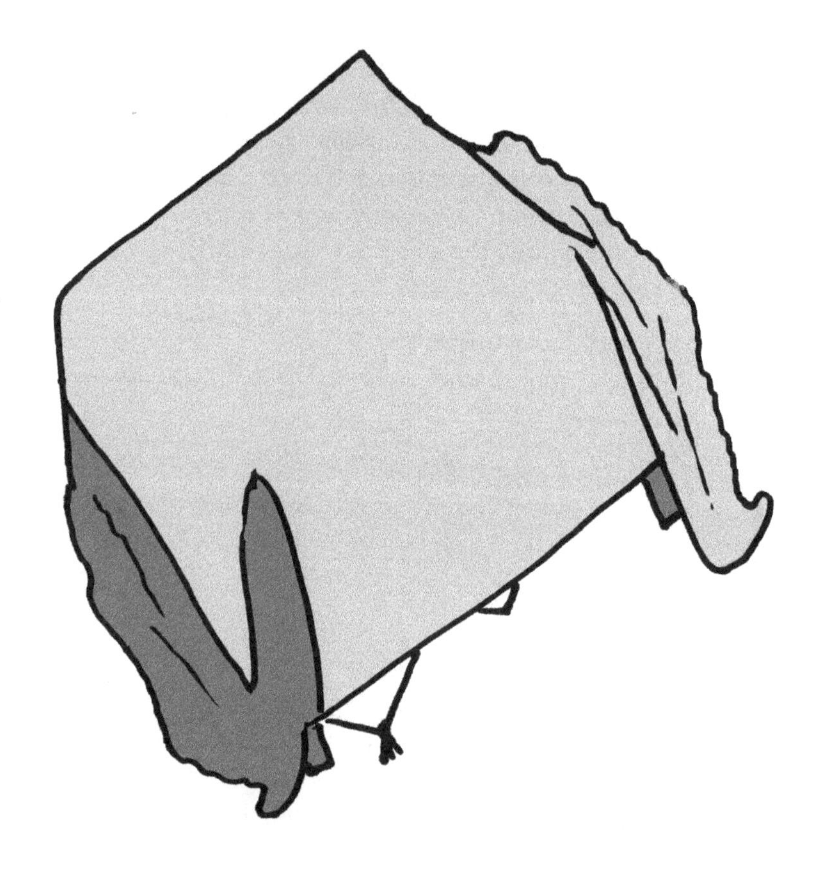

7

AHA!!!

"Yes, ten rows down, a million to go!" Rose exclaimed. Then she heard her mom calling her from the other room.

"Can you girls come in here for a moment?"

"Sure," Rose replied, and they both sighed and set aside their work.

"Oh, wait," Melanie said. "If we just leave it here, someone is bound to take it."

So they both picked up their projects and headed to her mom.

"Rose, Melanie, how would you girls like to have sleep over this weekend?" Rose's mom asked them with a smile.

"Yes!" they both exclaimed simultaneously.

Rose's mom picked her phone back up and typed something.

"Alright then. Melanie's mom needs us to keep both Melanie and Jerry this weekend. I knew you would love a sleepover."

Rose groaned. "Jerry too?"

"Yes, Rose, Jerry too."

"But that might help us catch whoever is stealing the yarn in the act, Jerry or not," Melanie comforted Rose.

Rose's mom gave them a sour look. "I don't want to hear about you girls framing poor Jerry for anything."

"We wouldn't be framing him if we catch him in the act," Rose defended herself.

"You would be if you set up him up."

"It would be a trap for the cat or dog too," Melanie said.

Rose's mom just narrowed her eyes as they head back to the craft room.

"Let's make a plan," Melanie suggested as they sat back down to work on their knitting.

Friday night, they set their plan in motion.

Melanie looked through a box of yarn balls for the perfect one.

Not yellow, she decided, since it was Jerry's favorite color. She held up a ball of purple yarn and asked Rose, "How about this one?"

"Sure," Rose replied, not looking up from another box of knitting supplies.

Yellow, she decided. "Is Jerry's favorite color yellow? I have these great yellow knitting needles."

Then she noticed Melanie setting down her favorite ball of yarn. "Wait a second, not that one."

"But you said sure," Melanie said defensively. "And not yellow needles, that is Jerry's favorite color, and we don't want our moms mad at us."

"What about blue?" Rose asked.

"Perfect," Melanie replied, "how about red yarn?"

"Sure," Rose answered with a smile.

"Now what?" Melanie asked as she looks at their trap.

"I'll go ask my mom if we can sleep in the craft room tonight. Jerry will be in the living room on the other side of the house."

"Let's make a table fort so that the suspect doesn't see us watching," Rose suggested.

"Perfect," Melanie replied. "I'll go grab my sleeping bag and pillow."

Rose draped a blanket over the table and stuffed her sleeping bag inside the table fort.

The two girls crouched down and settled in for the night of watching.

"I'll take the first shift," Rose volunteered.

"Well, I'm not tired yet, and besides, it would be better if we both see the crime in action."

"I don't know if I can stay up that long," Rose sighed.

"Don't worry, I'll keep you up." Melanie gives her an evil grin, then grabs some cards from her backpack. They both giggle.

Once the giggling subsides, Rose asks Melanie, "Do you want to play Go Fish or Crazy Eights?"

"Crazy Eights, it's quieter and we don't want to make too much noise."

Click. The light goes out.

"Aaauh," Melanie gasped. "We can't play in the dark!"

"We also can't see the yarn. I'll ask if we can leave the hall light on, and I'll grab a flashlight for the game."

"MOOOM!" Rose crawls out and runs after her mom. Thump. "I'M OKAY!" Rose exclaimed as she bounced off the wall.

The hall light came back on. "What do you need?" her moms asked.

"Can you leave the hall light on?" she asked her mom.

"Okaaay," her mom replies. "Is that all?"

Rose just grinned, then grabbed a flashlight off the hall table and headed back to Melanie.

They played a few rounds of cards when they finally heard something.

Melanie holds her finger up to her mouth and peeked around the blanket.

Rose crawled to the other corner and peeked out too.

Thump, something jumped up on the table, slid across, and landed on the the other side.

"What was that?" Melanie whispered.

"I don't know," Rose whispered back. "Maybe the cat?"

When they didn't see anything near the yarn, they settled back in, and then Mr. Whiskers slipped in and curled up with them. "Yep, must have been the cat." The two girls giggled.

"Well, if Mr. Whiskers is guilty, then I don't think we will catch him in the act tonight," Melanie whispered after petting the cat for a few minutes.

"The night's not over. Jerry could still get caught," Rose whispered back when she saw a flash of brown out of the corner of her eye.

Rose moved back over to peek out again, holding her finger up to her mouth. This time she saw a large dark shape blocking the light. When it moved again, the yarn was gone, so Rose got up and headed in that direction. She saw Ruffbert with the ball in his mouth as he slipped into the hallway.

"I can't believe it. Ruffbert did it!" Melanie exclaimed in a hushed way so that she wouldn't wake up Rose's parents.

8

Finally Finishing the Scarf

The next morning, the two girls sat at the breakfast table, explaining to Rose's mom what they saw.

"We followed Ruffbert, and you won't believe what happened," Rose said.

Melanie took over. "He took the ball upstairs to the cat tree and—"

"—and played with it for a few minutes," Rose continued.

"Then picked it up and put on the top of the cat tree!" Melanie bounced in her seat.

"Framing Mr. Whiskers!" Rose finished.

"Sounds like you two had an adventure," Rose's mom put in.

"Ahhh, I missed it," Jerry cried.

"But we proved it wasn't you," Melanie smiled at her brother.

Rose sighed and shook her head in disappointment.

"But what are we going to do to keep it from happening again?" Rose's mom asked the girls.

"Ooh, lets look around the craft room and see what we can find," Rose suggested.

The girls excused themselves and went to the craft room to brainstorm.

"I know, we can think while we knit." Melanie grabbed her project and settled down to work.

Several rows later, Melanie stopped and looked up. "I know, what if we knit a bag to keep the knitting in?" Melanie suggested.

"What keeps the dog from just taking the bag?" Rose shook her head no.

"We could hang it up?" Melanie replied.

"Well, that would take too long. We need a solution now," Rose said.

"How about one of those bags." Melanie points to a pile of bags shoved on a shelf.

"That sounds good, let's find the perfect one."

"Wait, I'm almost done!" Melanie exclaimed.

"Really?" Rose looks closer at Melanie's project.

"Wow!"

"I'd better catch up!"

Once they both finished their projects, they held up two scarves and grinned at each other. Done!

"Now we can go tell my mom," Rose said.

They got up and went to find her. It only took a minute to pitch the idea.

"Good idea, girls, now we just need to remember to use it."

"Easy peasy." Rose grinned.

"Only one thing left to do," Melanie declared.

"What?" Rose and her mom both asked.

"Write 'Case Closed' on the file!" Jerry shouted.

ABOUT THE AUTHOR

Charlotte Mae Mokry is 11 years old and loves to tell stories. She is the youngest member of her family and the second member to become a published author. Her imagination is wild and takes her on some very creative adventures. When she was 9, with the help of her mom—a children's book author and illustrator—she wrote her first book. They hope you have enjoyed this second book as much as they enjoyed writing it. Will there be more? We hope so.

CPSIA information can be obtained
at www.ICGtesting.com
Printed in the USA
BVHW032004150223
658591BV00004B/125

9 781951 521882